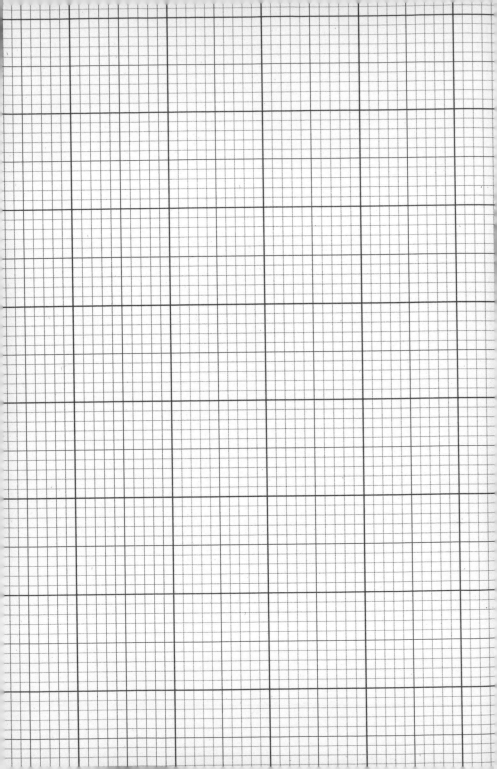

THIS NOTEBOOK BELONGS TO:

Ada

OTHER BOOKS BY
ANDREA BEATY AND
DAVID ROBERTS

Iggy Peck, Architect

Rosie Revere, Engineer

Ada Twist, Scientist

*Rosie Revere's Big Project
Book for Bold Engineers*

*Iggy Peck's Big Project
Book for Amazing Architects*

*Ada Twist's Big Project
Book for Stellar Scientists*

*Rosie Revere and the
Raucous Riveters*

ADA TWIST

AND THE PERILOUS PANTS

by Andrea Beaty   illustrated by David Roberts

AMULET BOOKS
NEW YORK

Cataloging-in-Publication Data has been applied for and may be obtained from the Library of Congress.

ISBN 978-1-4197-3422-9

Text copyright © 2019 Andrea Beaty
Illustrations copyright © 2019 David Roberts
Book design by Chad W. Beckerman

Printed and bound in China
11 10 9 8 7 6 5

Amulet Books are available at special discounts when purchased in quantity for premiums and promotions as well as fundraising or educational use. Special editions can also be created to specification. For details, contact specialsales@abramsbooks.com or the address below.

ABRAMS The Art of Books
195 Broadway, New York, NY 10007
abramsbooks.com

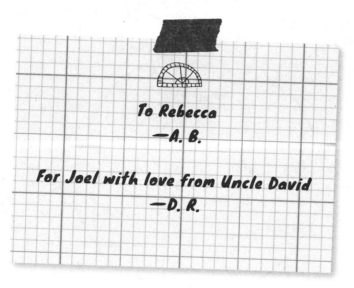

To Rebecca
—A. B.

For Joel with love from Uncle David
—D. R.

Chicken

Egg

What came first

Chicken or egg ???

CHAPTER 1

Ada Twist woke to the smell of breakfast. She jumped out of bed and followed her nose to the kitchen where her father was cooking eggs with onions. He was also boiling two dozen eggs for egg salad.

"There you are!" he said. "Hugs in a second. Eggs first!"

"Everyone knows that chickens come first!" said Ada.

Her dad laughed. It was the same joke Ada

made every time her dad cooked eggs for breakfast. They were being goofy, but the age-old question still made her wonder: Which came first, the chicken or the egg?

Someday, thought Ada, I'll do an experiment to find out!

"Hugs come first over here!" said Ada's mom, who was sitting at the table by two coffee mugs.

Ada hugged her mother. The smell of her mom's sweet perfume mingled with the bitter scent of steaming-hot coffee. The mix was one of the best smells in the world to Ada. She smiled.

"My turn," said Mr. Twist, setting the bowl of eggs and onions on the table.

Ada took a step toward him but stopped suddenly. The strong, bitter aroma of coffee above her mom's mug filled her nostrils. But her dad's mug of coffee had no smell at all. Ada leaned closer and sniffed again.

Nothing.

Ada pulled out her notebook and jotted a question: Why does Mom's coffee have a smell but not Dad's?

Ada's dad smiled and hugged her.

"Did you already find a mystery before breakfast?" he asked.

Ada grinned. Questions filled her mind as she looked at the coffee mugs. The day had just begun, and she already had a mystery to solve. As a scientist, nothing made her happier.

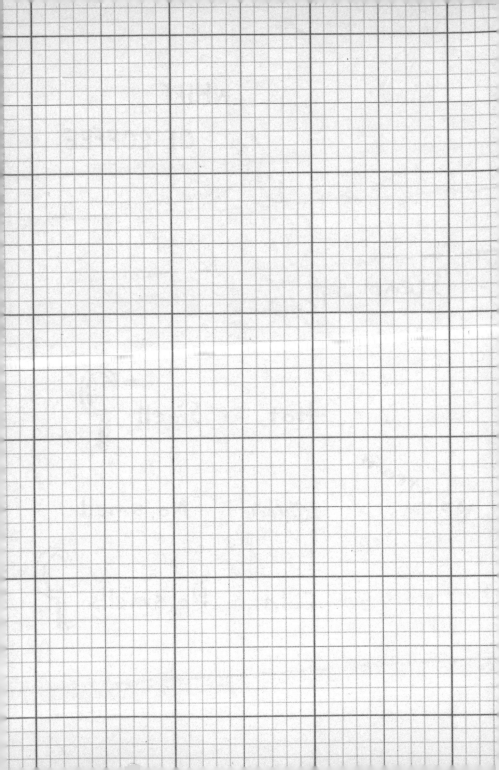

CHAPTER 2

Ada pulled the tape measure out of her pocket. She always kept one handy. She measured the distance from her nose to the top of her mother's coffee mug. She bent closer and closer to the mug, sniffing, measuring, and taking notes. She could smell the coffee from her mom's mug from twelve centimeters away. She repeated the steps with her dad's coffee mug. But she could not smell anything from his mug until her nose was only four centimeters away. Even then, the scent was faint.

"Your coffee is broken, Dad!" said Ada. "It doesn't smell!"

"Keep investigating," said Mrs. Twist. "You'll figure it out."

Ada knew that using all her senses was a great way to gather data.

Ada looked carefully at the mugs. Steam rose over her mom's mug like wispy smoke. Ada placed her right hand over the steam and her palm became damp. She placed her left hand over her dad's mug. Her left hand stayed dry.

Finally, Ada touched her mom's mug. It was hot. Her dad's mug was icy cold and a little damp.

"Zowie!" said Ada.

Her dad laughed and picked up his mug and took a drink.

"It's iced coffee," he said. "But the ice melted so it looks like the hot stuff."

"And speaking of hot," said Mrs. Twist, "can we eat while our eggs are still hot stuff?"

While Ada ate, more questions swirled around in her mind. What makes hot coffee hot? What makes steam? Why does it go up? Why was Dad's mug damp on the outside? Why does hot coffee smell more than cold coffee? Do other things smell stronger when they are hot than when they are cold?

Every question gave her two more questions. And each of those questions led her to four!

Just then, Ada's brother, Arthur, came into the kitchen carrying his tennis racket and his tennis shoes. As he passed Ada, a toe-curling stink whacked her right in the nose.

Zowie! thought Ada.

An idea popped into her brain. She could do an experiment!

"I wonder . . ." she said, and she tapped her chin.

A look of panic crossed Arthur's face. A similar look crossed her cat, Bunsen Burner's, face. Bunsen darted out of the room. Arthur pointed at Ada.

"Ada's doing that tapping thing!" said Arthur, who had seen that look on her face before.

It usually led to something messy happening. Or worse.

"Hey, Arthur!" Ada said eagerly. "Do you want to help me do some science?"

"No!" said Arthur. "And don't use my stuff! Remember what Mom and Dad said?"

Arthur loved his sister and he loved science

experiments, too. But he didn't love Ada's experiments when they used his stuff. He was still getting pudding out of his Lego blocks from the time Ada tested what made things sticky. After that, his parents made rules about how Ada could conduct her experiments, but sometimes she forgot. Rule No. 1 was: Don't take Arthur's things without his permission.

"Of course, I remember," said Ada. "I wrote it down. See?"

Ada flipped open her notebook and held it up for him.

"I always write down important things so I won't forget," Ada said.

Arthur frowned and plopped into a chair. As he ate his breakfast, he watched Ada warily. But Ada was too busy working to notice. She scribbled notes and grinned. She loved having a question to explore. It was a mystery! A riddle! A puzzle! A quest! This was the moment that Ada loved best.

It was science time!

Read
Question
ThinK?

① What are smells ?
② What are gases ?
③ What is **Air** ?

CHAPTER 3

Ada spent the next two hours reading her science books. She needed to know more about air and gases and about heat and smells. Research helped her understand what scientists had already figured out. It gave her some answers to her questions and then led to other questions to explore.

AIR! What's Up with That?
by Dr. Penelope H. Dee, PhD

What is air?

Air is the clear gas that surrounds the Earth. It is a mix of many other gases, dust particles, and water molecules. Most of air is nitrogen (78%), oxygen (21%), and other trace gases, including carbon dioxide and helium, which make up less than a tenth of 1%.

We call the air around Earth the *atmosphere*. Gravity pulls the atmosphere toward the center of the Earth. (That's why it doesn't just fly off into space.) Atmospheric pressure is the force of the air pushing against objects. Atmospheric pressure is highest at the Earth's surface, because gravity is pulling all the air above it toward the center of the planet. (That's a lot of air!) There is less and less air as you travel from the planet's surface toward space. So, there is less pressure!

It's like being in an ocean. When you float near the top of the ocean, there is only a small amount of water pushing down on you. When you swim at the bottom of the ocean, all the weight of the water between you and the ocean's surface is pushing down on you. That is much heavier!

What are gases?

Gases expand to fill the space that is available. Gases expand when they are heated, and gases shrink and become denser when they are cooled.

Gas molecules move faster when they are hot than when they are cold. Gas molecules travel until they bounce off other molecules. Then they change directions and keep traveling. Diffusion is when gas molecules continue to spread out as far as they can from the other molecules.

What are smells?

Smells are just molecules that reach the special cells in your nose. These cells are called olfactory receptor neurons. When a chemical molecule hits them, they send a message to your brain. Your brain figures out if the smell is familiar, pleasant, nasty, or has other traits.

Ada loved reading about air, molecules, and smells. But she wanted to do something.

I know, she thought. I'll try to answer one question: Does a thing smell more when it is hot than cold?

From her observations and from her research, Ada had a strong idea that she wanted to test. She had a hypothesis.

Ada's hypothesis: If Arthur has two identical shoes but one is hot and one is cold, the hot one will stink more.

Perfect, thought Ada. Let the science experiment begin. Status: Project Underway. P.U.!

NOTES
&
OBSERVATIONS
&
QUESTIONS

① I tested popsicles for quality. A+ (Need more popsicles.)

② How many ants does it take to eat a popsicle? 127. (Need more popsicles.)

③ Squirrels like stinky shoes.

④ Gray squirrel = fast. Gray squirrel + stinky shoe = fast. Gray squirrel + stinky shoe + scientist hanging onto shoe = slow.

⑤ Mom hides popsicles behind frozen peas.

⑥ How do ants find melted popsicles in stinky shoes?

⑦ Why is it cooler in the shade? Is all shade the same?

⑧ Did Arthur have stinky baby feet?

CHAPTER 4

It was very hot in Ada's yard. Ada had been working for an hour and had already tested her hypothesis seven times. Each time, she took notes. She wanted to try the experiment ten or even twenty times to get lots of information to study.

Time for test number eight. Ada Twist put her notebook and pencil in her pocket. She pulled the bandana down over her eyes. She twirled around three times and stopped.

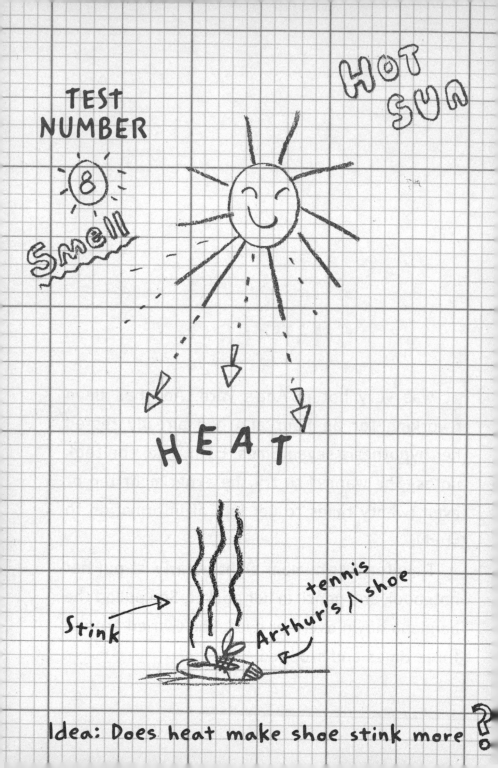

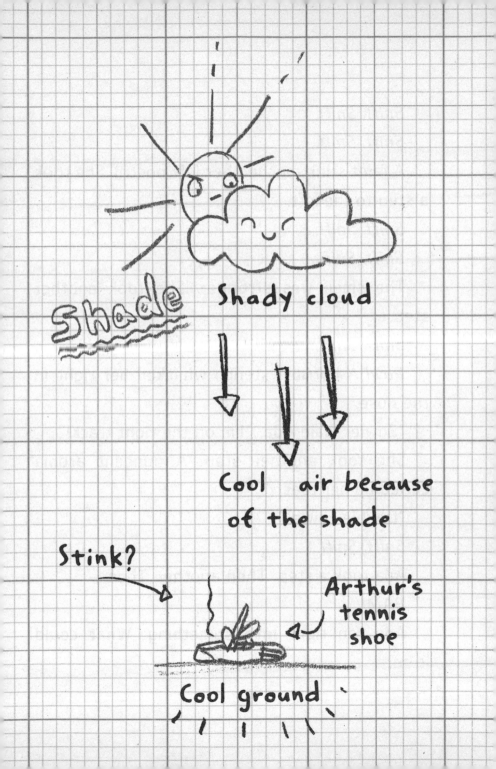

Sniff. Sniff.

Sniff. Sniff.

A faint stink reached her left nostril. She took a step to the left.

Sniff. Sniff.

Sniff. Sniff.

The smell was stronger. She took another step.

Sniff. Sniff.

Pow! A horrible stench whacked her right in the nose.

"Zowie!" said Ada. "I'm on the right track!"

She took another step. A pungent aroma curled up her toes.

"Double zowie!"

Sniff. Sniff.

Ada took a step. Then another. Then—
BAM!

Ada ran right into something. What could it be?

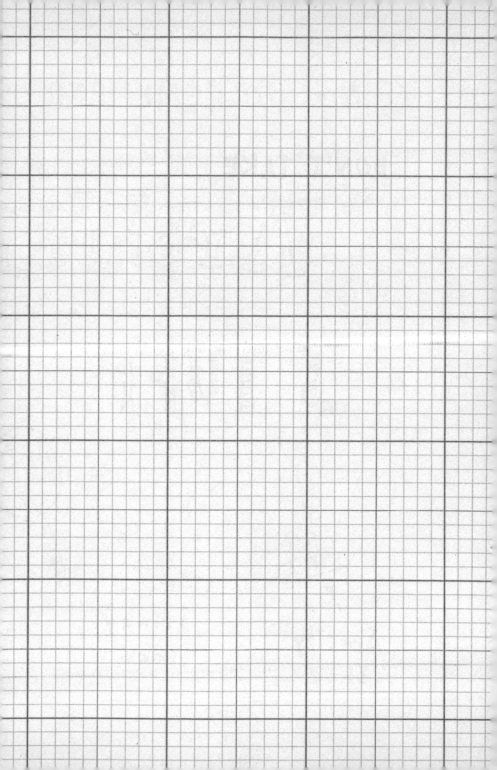

THINGS TO REMEMBER

DON'T TAKE

Arthur's

STUFF

Smelly shoe

Stinky sock

CHAPTER 5

Ada poked the thing with her finger. It was softer than a tree.

Poke. Poke.

Poke. Poke.

"Cut it out!"

It was noisier than a tree!

Ada peeked under the bandana. She saw a pair of feet in striped socks. She knew those socks!

It was Arthur. He stood there tapping his foot and pointing at his shoe.

"Hi, Arthur!" said Ada, taking off the bandana. "Did you come to help?"

"No," he said in a cranky voice. "I want my tennis shoes back! Stop using my stuff!"

"But you have the stinkiest feet!" said Ada.

She meant it as a compliment. Arthur did not take it as a compliment.

He frowned and tapped his foot faster.

"Look!" said Ada, holding up the notebook. "The hot shoe is stinkier than the cold one! I thought it would be!"

She smiled hopefully at Arthur, who frowned harder and crammed his right foot into the cold shoe.

"ICK!" yelled Arthur and he pulled his foot out.

A glob of frozen purple popsicle stuck to his sock.

"Why is there a purple popsicle in my shoe?" he asked.

"Because we didn't have any red ones," said Ada. "Do you think a red popsicle would make the shoe colder than a purple one? I could do an experiment to find out!"

Ada jotted a note. Arthur rolled his eyes.

He picked up the left shoe and three hard-boiled eggs tumbled out.

"That's the hot shoe," said Ada. "The boiled eggs heated it really fast!"

Ada could see that Arthur was not happy. Maybe he didn't understand what she was trying to do. She tried to explain.

"The hot molecules go really fast and bounce around," said Ada, "then the smells go like this—"

Ada pointed wildly this way and that and added a high-pitched *ZOOP! ZOOP!* noise for special effect.

"And the cold molecules are slow," said Ada.

She pointed slowly this way and that and added a low-pitched *FSHOO! FSHOO!* sound.

"But they're all silent," said Ada, repeating the gestures silently. "And they're all way faster than my fingers. And they are really tiny. There's no way you could see them! And . . ."

Arthur made an *UGH!* kind of sound and rolled his eyes. He grabbed his sneakers by the laces and trudged back toward the house.

"There were lots of smell molecules in there," said Ada. "They hit my nose and . . . then the receptor cells and . . . and then my brain goes . . . *ZOWIE*! And—here! I'll draw you a picture!"

Arthur kept walking.

"Your stinky feet were made for science!" Ada yelled as Arthur reached the house.

The door slammed behind him.

"Hmm," said Ada.

Arthur didn't get it. Ada knew what she wanted him to understand, but when she tried to explain, all her ideas seemed to burst out at the same time and then everything got jumbled. Why did that always happen to Ada?

Ada sat beneath the tree and thought. Why did all her ideas want to get out at the same time? Did other people's ideas do that? Could she do an experiment to find out? Could her friends Rosie Revere and Iggy Peck help her?

Ada smiled. She loved working with her friends

and they always had great ideas. That would be a fun project to work on one day. The thought of it made her feel better.

Ada went back to her notes. She was happy with the results of her stink experiment. She had hoped for more data, but even with only eight tries instead of dozens, she could see a pattern. The data seemed to confirm her hypothesis that the hot shoe was the stinkiest. But she needed more data to be sure.

Ada was about to design a new hot-stink experiment when a bird chirped in the tree above her.

"Uh-oh!" Ada said. "I almost forgot! It's birding time."

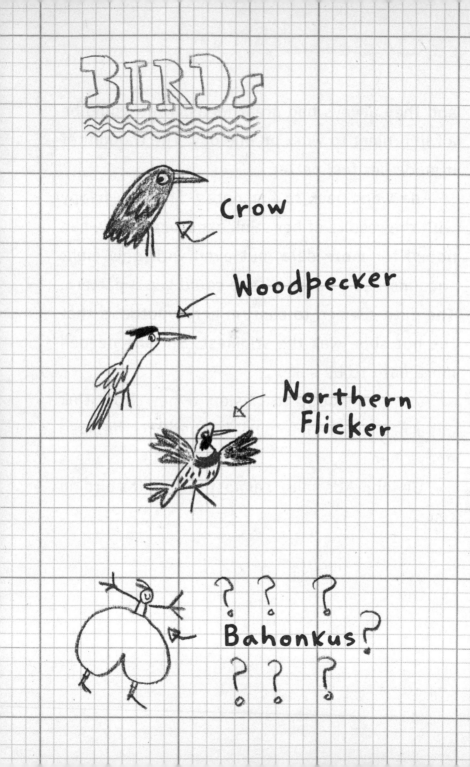

CHAPTER 6

Ada grabbed her binoculars and came back to the tree. The Great Backyard Bird Count was only a few weeks away. Every year on the same day, Ada joined people around the world who counted birds in their own yards. Then, they all shared the data they collected. That data told scientists how many birds there were and where they lived and where they traveled.

Ada practiced identifying birds every day. She studied pictures and knew many birds by sight.

But she wanted to know bird calls, too. Ada listened to the birds in the tree.

CAW–CAW–CAW.

"Crow!" she said.

KNOCK–KNOCK–KNOCK.

"Woodpecker!"

TAP–TAP–TAP.

"Northern Flicker."

OOOOOOOOOOPS!

"Oops?" said Ada. "I don't know that one!"

She listened again.

OH NOOOOOOOOO!

"'Oh no'?" said Ada. "What kind of bird sounds like that?"

She looked through her binoculars.

"Zowie!" said Ada. "That's not a bird! That's not a plane! That's . . . a bahonkus!"

Ada was right. It was a bahonkus. A very big bahonkus and it belonged to a very skinny man with a very big mustache and a very, very big pair of pants.

They were the biggest pants Ada had ever seen. They were fluffy and puffy and they were floating above the tree!

And that wasn't just any man. That was—

"UNCLE NED!"

Ada turned to see her friends Rosie Revere and Iggy Peck running toward her. They were shouting and waving their arms.

"Stop that uncle!" yelled Rosie.

Ada looked up. A long rope dangled from

Uncle Ned's waist. It was snagged on a branch at the top of the tree. Rosie and Iggy skidded to a halt next to Ada. They were out of breath and their faces were bright red.

"Hi!" said Ada.

"Thanks for catching Uncle Ned!" said Rosie. "We've been chasing him all over Blue River Creek!"

"Why is he flying around?" asked Ada. "Is it an experiment? I love experiments! Is it an experiment about flying? Wind? Birds? Leaves? Clouds? Is it about weather? Is it—"

"It's about getting me down!" yelled Uncle Ned.

"We're trying!" said Rosie.

"Why are his pants floating?" asked Ada. "Are they filled with gas?"

"I heard that," called Uncle Ned.

"They're filled with helium gas, which is lighter than air," said Rosie. "I made them for him when I was younger."

"Sometimes, he wears them on a walk," said Iggy. "Though I guess it's a float, because someone else is doing the walking. They hold the rope so Uncle Ned doesn't fly off."

Flying around in helium pants was dangerous. It was hazardous. It was perilous. It was also really cool.

"Uncle Fred was holding the rope today," said Rosie. "And then he saw a—"

"Let me guess," said Ada. "Did Uncle Fred see a snake?"

Rosie nodded. Everyone knew her Uncle Fred. He was the zookeeper in Blue River Creek. Everyone also knew that Uncle Fred loved snakes. And they loved him. He found them everywhere he went. It always led to trouble.

"He picked up the snake," Rosie said, "and—"

"And he let go of the rope!" said Ada. "What kind of snake was it?"

"An annoying one!" yelled Uncle Ned. "Get me down from here!"

Feather

Foot

= Ha Ha
Hee Hee

Tickle

What is ticklish?

Why are humans ticklish?

CHAPTER 7

W hile you're up there," yelled Ada. "Do you see any birds? I'm trying to count them."

"I see a very hungry-looking crow!" said Uncle Ned. "I don't like the way it's staring at me . . . nice birdie . . . nope . . . get off my head . . . hey! That tickles . . . hee-hee . . . cut it out! . . . Ha-ha! . . . Hee-hee! . . . I'm ticklish! . . . Ha-ha, hee-hee, ha-ha!"

Indeed, Uncle Ned was very ticklish. All of Rosie's aunts and uncles were. And once they got laughing, it was hard for them to stop. Uncle Ned tried to swat the bird away, but he was laughing too hard.

"Hee-hee! Ha-ha!"

Meanwhile, the kids brainstormed ideas. They often thought up ideas together and helped one another with projects. They spent so much time answering questions that Ada's Aunt Bernice gave them a nickname. She called them The Questioneers!

The Questioneers thought and thought.

"I could make a gadget to help him steer

the helium pants," said Rosie, who was an engineer. "But how could we get it to him?"

"I know!" said Iggy, who was an architect. "We could build a tree house and climb up to him! Or we could make the Leaning Tower of Pizza Boxes! Do you have fifty pizza boxes?"

Ada shook her head.

"It doesn't matter now," she said.

"Why not?" asked Iggy.

"Just look," said Ada.

Iggy and Rosie looked up. They saw lots of branches. They saw lots of leaves. They saw a hungry crow. But they did NOT see a pair of perilous, puffy pants or a skinny man with a very big mustache.

Uncle Ned was gone!

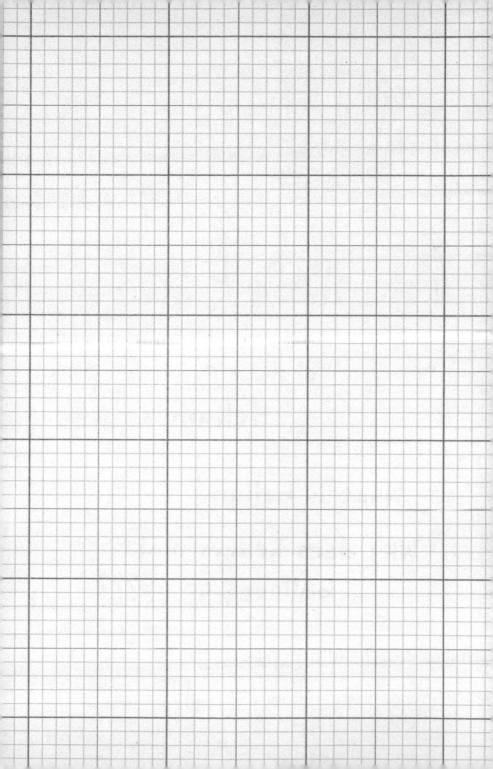

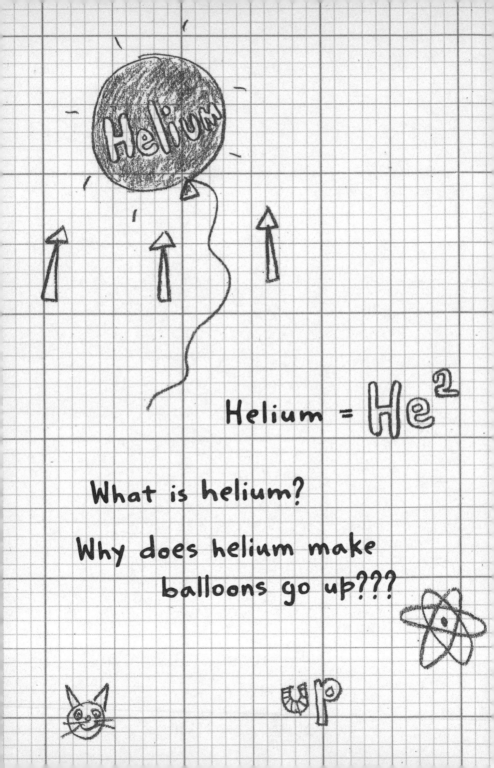

Helium = He^2

What is helium?

Why does helium make
 balloons go up???

up

CHAPTER 8

The three kids looked this way and that way. There was no sign of Uncle Ned or his perilous pants.

"Do you think the crow got him?" asked Iggy.

"He could be anywhere!" said Rosie. She was worried.

"Let's think like scientists," said Ada calmly. "Let's start with questions."

Rosie looked up.

"What if he went straight up to space?" she asked.

Ada tapped her chin and thought a moment.

"I don't think Uncle Ned could get up to space," said Ada. "I was reading about gases in my book. Helium is a gas and it follows all the rules of gases. Gas molecules spread out in every direction to fill the space around them."

Ada started pointing and making hand gestures and sound effects. She wanted to tell Rosie and Iggy all the things she had read about gases. The thoughts were crowding her brain and fighting to get out all at once.

Then, Ada stopped. She was doing the same thing she had done when she tried to explain her experiment to Arthur. That didn't work so well. Maybe now was the time to try something new.

"I'll show you!" said Ada.

Ada took a deep breath and pulled out her notebook. Sometimes it helped her when she sketched in her notebook and then explained as she went.

"Helium is a gas, so it follows the rules of all gases," she said. "Gas molecules spread out to fill the space around them. So the helium molecules are filling all the space inside the pants. They push on the material with enough force to make the pants puffy. See?"

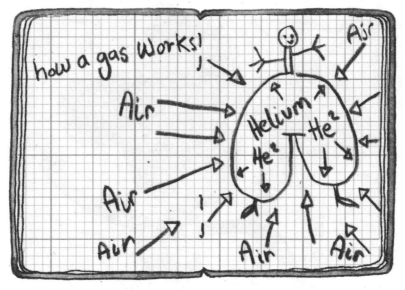

Using pictures made explaining things so much easier. Ada's ideas seemed to get in line and come out in the right order. And it was working. Rosie and Iggy nodded as she explained, though they still looked a little confused. Ada continued.

"While the gas molecules are pushing outward," she said, "the air above and around Uncle Ned is also trying to spread out and is pushing on the outside of the pants."

"So?" said Iggy.

"So," said Ada, "the pants are just a balloon. The gas inside is trying to expand but the strength of the balloon and the pressure of the air outside the balloon keeps it from stretching too far."

"Okay," said Iggy.

"Then," said Ada, "if Uncle Ned goes up, up, up, there is less air above him and around him, so there are fewer molecules to push on the outside of the pants. But there is the same amount of pressure from the helium molecules *inside* the pants."

Rosie jumped in.

"So . . . the helium in the pants can expand more because there is more pressure on the inside of the pants than the outside of the pants," said Rosie.

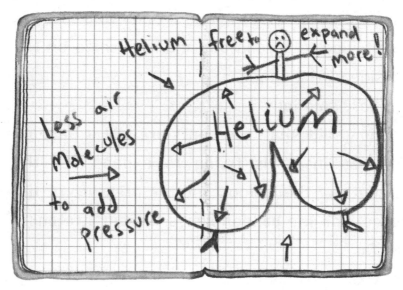

"Right!" said Ada, who was trying to remember what she had read. "So . . ." she said as she tapped on her chin, "Uncle Ned's pants will keep expanding!"

"And?" asked Rosie.

"And they will get bigger and bigger and . . ." said Ada.

"And?" asked Rosie nervously.

Ada gulped.

"And what?" asked Rosie.

Ada took a deep breath. A worried look crossed her face.

"What?" asked Rosie.

"The pressure inside the pants will be much stronger than the pressure outside," said Ada, "and . . . they'll pop."

"Oh no!" Rosie gasped. "Uncle Ned will fall from space!"

"No. Actual space is sixty miles up!" Ada said. "His pants would explode way before then!"

Rosie's eyes got wide.

"Oh no!" said Ada. "I'm not explaining it right. I didn't mean to upset you. I just meant that he wouldn't float that far up . . ."

But Rosie was upset. She looked at the sky and a tiny tear welled up at the corner of her eye.

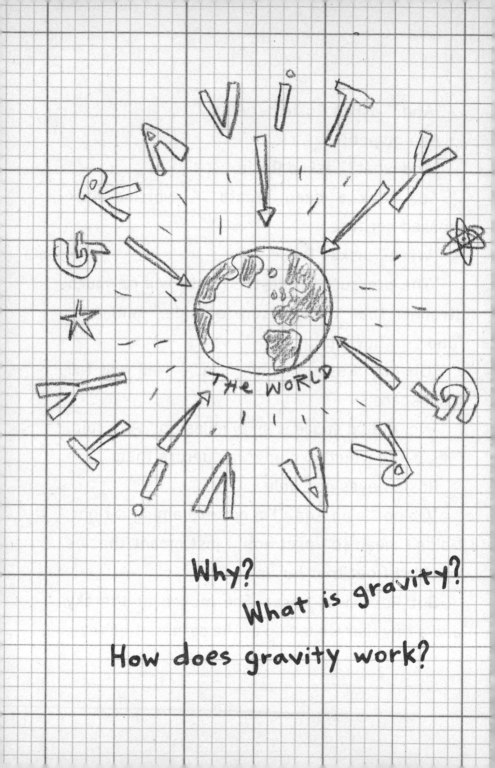

GRAVITY

THE WORLD

Why?

What is gravity?

How does gravity work?

CHAPTER 9

Ada didn't mean to upset Rosie. How could she explain? She thought for a moment. She tried a new approach.

"What happened when Uncle Fred let go of Uncle Ned's rope?" asked Ada.

"He floated away," said Iggy.

"Okay, but *exactly* how did he do it?" asked Ada. "Did he pop straight up? Did he hover over the ground? Did he bob up and down like a fishing float? Did he blow away in a straight line? Did he zig? Did he zag?"

"I don't know," said Rosie.

She was more upset than ever. Ada gave her friend a hug and smiled.

"Just tell me what you saw," said Ada kindly. "*Exactly* what did you observe? If we think like scientists, we'll figure out which way he went. Then we'll find Uncle Ned and rescue him. We won't give up."

"Rosie," said Iggy, "you always tell us not to give up. Remember?"

Rosie smiled and took a deep breath to calm herself.

"Stop and think!" she said.

It was advice that Aunt Rose often gave her. It helped her to focus when she had a problem to solve.

"Okay," said Rosie. "The first thing that happened was that Uncle Fred let go of the rope."

"Then Uncle Ned popped straight up into the air," said Iggy.

"How far?" asked Ada.

"Twice as high as our roof," said Rosie. "Then he stopped!"

"Yay!" said Ada. "That's good news!"

"Uncle Ned didn't think so," said Iggy.

"It's great news!" said Ada. "I'll show you."

Ada sketched another picture. It showed Uncle Ned in the air with lots of arrows going this way and that around him.

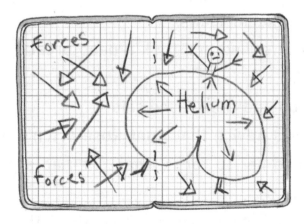

"Each arrow shows a force," said Ada. "A force is how energy acts on an object. Forces can come from all directions. For example, Uncle Ned is the object and the forces are the air pushing down on him from above. And gravity pulling him toward the center of the Earth!"

"But the air that he's floating on is a force pushing up," said Iggy. "It's like a boat on water!"

"Yes!" said Ada. "Those arrows pointing up show buoyancy!"

"AND there's the lift of the helium as it tries to rise above the heavier air!" said Rosie.

"So, the pants want to go up, up, up," said Ada, "but the other forces keep him down. We will find Uncle Ned where the forces balance. Right now, that's twice as high as Rosie's roof!"

"That's a long way from space," said Rosie.

She sounded calmer.

"It sure is," said Ada.

"Okay," said Iggy. "What about the wind? It's a force pushing him from the side."

"If Uncle Ned is gone with the wind," said Ada, "let's follow the wind!"

THINGS TO DO TODAY

Find out

What is **Air ?**

Air currents

Cool
air

Warm
air

Cloud

What is
air flow ?

Earth

CHAPTER 10

Ada scraped a small handful of fine dust from the ground. She held out her hand and dumped the dust. The heavy bits fell straight down, but the finest dust blew toward Blue River Creek. Ada took her compass from her pocket. (She always had one handy.) The compass needle pointed north.

The three friends ran north. With any luck, Uncle Ned's rope would snag on one of the tall trees that lined the river. Then, they could figure

out how to get him down. The Questioneers ran past the school and the library. They were passing the City Hall when Ada screeched to a stop.

WHOA!

Iggy and Rosie crashed into Ada. The three friends tumbled into a heap.

"Ouch," said Rosie.

"Why did you stop?" asked Iggy.

"Look at the weather vane!" said Ada.

Rosie and Iggy looked at the copper weather vane at the tip top of City Hall. The arrow pointed north toward the river.

"We're going that way," said Rosie.

"That's the problem!" said Ada. "Weather vanes are shaped like wedges, so they always point where the wind is coming FROM!"

"That means the wind is blowing south!" said Iggy. "But the dust blew north."

"The dust is close to the ground," said Ada.

"Uncle Ned is high in the air like the weather vane!"

Iggy looked confused.

"Air flows in currents like water in the ocean," said Ada. "There can be currents that go different directions. So, the air down low can blow a different way than the air up high."

"What if Uncle Ned already blew out of town?" asked Rosie. "What if we never find him?"

Suddenly, a red fire truck swooped around the corner and zoomed down the street.

HONK! HONK!

WOOOOOOOO-WOOOOOOOO-WOOOOOOOO!

HONK! HONK!

"I think someone just did!" said Iggy.

A short, zebra-striped bus also rounded the corner and stopped in front of the kids. It was Uncle Fred in the Zoo Bus.

"Hop in!" he said. "We found Uncle Ned!"

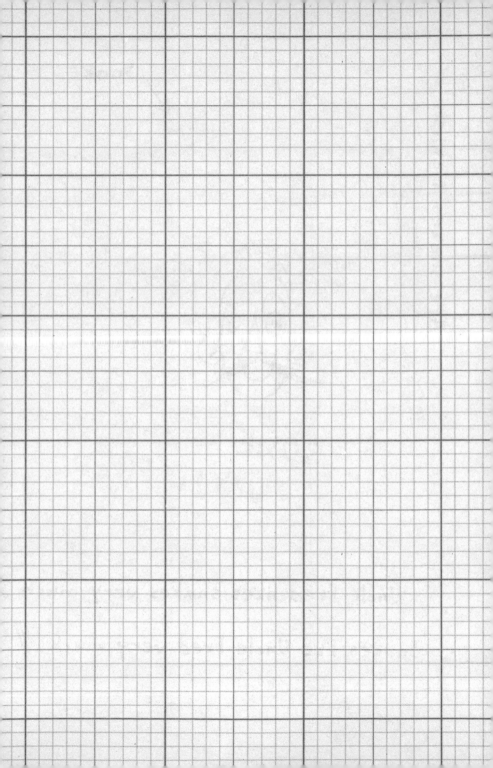

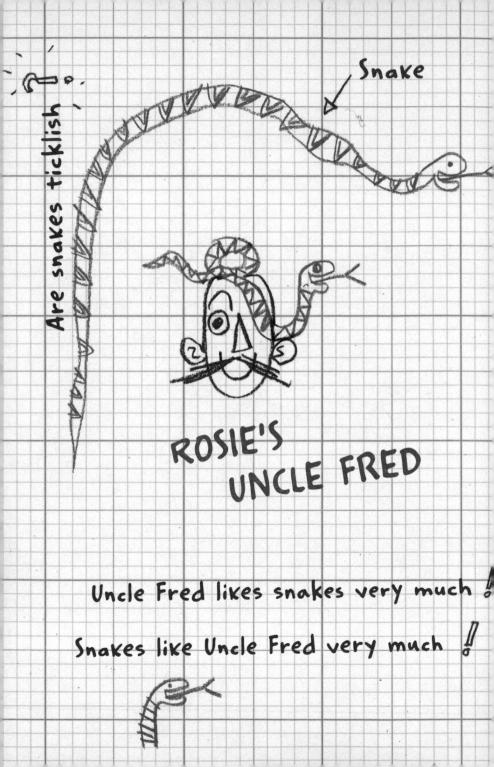

CHAPTER II

Uncle Fred hit the gas. They zoomed after the fire truck, which turned another corner and stopped behind the old jeep factory. Bee and Beau, from Blue River Creek's volunteer fire department, jumped out of the fire truck. Rosie, Ada, Iggy, and Uncle Fred tumbled out of the bus.

It was the factory where Rosie's neighbor Mrs. Lu built jeeps during World War II. The factory had been closed for years and most of the building was gone. Only three tall walls were left standing. They made a courtyard shaped like the letter U. The ground at the center was a small, empty parking lot covered with black asphalt. The blazing sun beat down on the hot, oily surface and the smell of tar filled the air. It was a stinky, thick smell that Ada did not like.

Uncle Ned was trapped in an air current that slowly whirled around inside the U-shaped area. The whirlwind picked up bits of dust and small leaves and lazily whirled them around and around, high in the air, with Uncle Ned.

"It's like in a river," said Iggy. "Where the water gets stuck by rocks and swirls around and around."

"I think they call that an eddy," said Rosie. "But how long can the whirlwind stay that way?"

Bee and Beau stretched out the fire truck's ladder. Rosie knew Bee and Beau because they were also the recyclers in Blue River Creek. They often left her boxes of recycled materials for her inventions.

"Hi, Rosie! Hi, Ada! Hi, Iggy!" they called.

Uncle Ned was trapped in the whirlwind near the top of the wall. He was too far from the wall to grab the bricks. And he was too far up to be reached by the ladder.

"Hi, Ned!" yelled Bee. "Give us a minute and we'll get you down!"

"Any time now, Bee!" said Uncle Ned as he whirled around and around. "I'm getting dizzy-izzy-izzy! Wooooo-oooooo-ooooo!"

Beau climbed to the top of the fire ladder and reached for the rope hanging from Uncle Ned's perilous pants. It dangled just out of Beau's grasp.

"Our ladder is too short!" yelled Beau. "Can you float lower?"

"Nooooooo-whooaaaa-whooaaa!" cried Ned. "I'm stuck!"

Bee stretched out the thick, white fire hose.

"I'll squirt you down with the hose!" she yelled.

"No!" said Rosie. "If he breaks out of this

eddy, he'll get pulled into a crosswind and float away!"

Ada looked carefully at the walls. The whirlwind kept Uncle Ned swirling in one spot. Iggy was right. It was like an eddy in a river. But Rosie was also right. If anything changed, Uncle Ned could fly away again. A squirt with the hose could be a disaster.

Word spread throughout Blue River Creek about Uncle Ned's perilous pants. Soon, a crowd gathered and watched. They cheered for the firefighters and The Questioneers and tried to keep Ned calm by singing songs and telling him jokes.

The jokes were a bad idea. Every time he started to laugh, his pants jiggled and he wobbled in the whirlwind. One big laugh might send him flying!

"Now that's a picture," said Barb Ross from the Happy Sapling Art Store. She pulled out a sketchpad and started to draw.

"Does he have a permit for that?" asked the mayor.

"What if we train an eagle to pop those perilous pants?" someone asked Uncle Fred.

The crowd liked that idea and clapped. Unfortunately, the eagle was still at the zoo. Meanwhile, three monkeys, four lemurs, and an ostrich ran in and out of the growing crowd while Uncle Fred tried to catch them.

A reporter from the *Blue River Reader* interviewed Uncle Ned and snapped some photos for the evening edition.

It was very exciting, but as everyone focused on Ned and his perilous pants, Ada Twist stood to the side, tapping her chin. She was thinking. Her mind was swirling with questions. Uncle Ned floated at exactly that height because of all the forces pulling him down and pushing him up. Could they change the forces to make Uncle Ned float lower so the firefighters could grab him? Could they weigh Uncle Ned down? Could the monkeys help? Could they really train an eagle to pop the pants? Would that make Uncle Ned zoom through the sky like a balloon losing its air? What if Uncle Ned hit something? Would he bounce?

The sun beat down on Ada and the stink of the asphalt rose up from the parking lot. It was a toe-curling stinky smell that made Ada feel a little woozy.

She shook her head to try to think. She tapped her chin again and scribbled notes. The hum of the crowd faded. There were so many questions to answer. So much to figure out. To Ada, the whole world felt like a big cartoon bubble filled with question marks.

She flipped through her notebook and looked at the pictures she had drawn for Rosie. All the forces working on Uncle Ned's perilous pants kept him in one spot. If any of the forces changed, Uncle Ned would move. The trick was making him move in the right direction.

Just like adding cargo to a ship changes how high it floats in the water, maybe they could change the way Uncle Ned's pants floated in the air? But how could they add cargo to his pants and what would that cargo be? How could they get anything to Uncle Ned when they couldn't reach him?

Suddenly, Ada had an idea. She popped out of her thought bubble and looked around. Rosie and Iggy were smiling at her.

"You have an idea," said Rosie, who knew that look on Ada's face.

"How do we help?" asked Iggy.

Ada scribbled some notes and showed them to her friends. Iggy and Rosie nodded. Rosie ran to Uncle Fred and whispered something in his ear. He nodded, too.

"We'll keep track of Uncle Ned in case he flies off again," said Iggy and Rosie.

Ada stuck her pencil behind her ear. She stuck her notebook in her pocket.

"Don't worry, Uncle Ned!" she yelled. "We'll get you down!"

"Can you make it soooooooo-oooooooo-ooooooon?" he yelled back. "I think that crow is coming back!"

Rosie pointed to a distant, dark cloud on the horizon.

"That's not all that's on its way," she said in a worried voice. "I don't think we have a lot of time before the wind changes. Hurry!"

Ada nodded. She jumped into the Zoo Bus, and once more, Uncle Fred hit the gas. They were off!

CHAPTER 12

Ada scrambled up the stairs to Arthur's room. A moment later, she ran down with her brother's tennis racquet and a large bag of tennis balls.

Mrs. Twist stopped her by the front door.

"Ada!" she said. "Are those Arthur's?"

"It's an emergency!" said Ada.

Ada's mother looked at her.

"Ada," she said calmly, "we've had this talk. You can't use your brother's things without his permission. If you need a racquet, use your own. Where is it?"

"Well . . ." said Ada.

"That's not a good answer," said her mother. "And you know it."

Ada did know it. What she didn't know was where she had left her own racquet. There were lots of possibilities. But there was no time to figure it out.

"Mom," Ada said. "I need to go now. This is really important!"

Mrs. Twist crossed her arms. "So is this," she said.

"But," said Ada, "the wind might change, and the whirlwind could collapse! And these tennis balls! They can add enough mass to the pants to offset the pants' buoyancy! So the forces balance at a lower height! Can't you see?"

"What?" asked Mrs. Twist.

She did not look happy.

Ada did not feel happy.

Why didn't her mother just understand what she was saying? She didn't have time to draw a picture. Maybe if she said it faster and louder!

Ada blurted out her ideas as fast and loud as she could. But her words jumbled and bumbled and fumbled. Some of them got left out altogether.

"Air pressure . . . jeep . . . buoyant force . . .

monkeys . . . gravity!" Ada said as fast as she could. "Tennis balls . . . LEAPING LEMURS!"

"ADA MARIE!"

Ada stopped talking. Her mother was frustrated and frazzled. She was mad.

And time was running out.

"Mom!" said Ada. "The downward forces have to be greater than the buoyant force or the pants will never sink, and—"

"Ada!" Mrs. Twist cut her off. "What did I tell you?"

Ada's parents were always telling her things, so Ada kept a list in her notebook. She flipped it open.

"The bathroom is not a science lab," she said.

"Not that," said her mother.

"The pantry is not an ant farm," said Ada.

"What else?"

"Don't put my toothbrush in the earthworm box," said Ada.

"Ada," her mother said in her trying-to-stay-calm voice, "what did we tell you about your brother's things?"

Ada's mother was upset, and it made Ada think of Rosie, who was upset, too. Rosie was scared and worried about Uncle Ned. Time was running out and no matter how fast Ada talked or how she tried to explain it to her mother, her mother didn't understand. What would Rosie do if Uncle Ned blew away? What if he blew away to a whole other country? What if Rosie never saw him again? It made Ada sad. Her heart turned to goo.

Ada stopped talking and stood quietly, not knowing what to do.

"Ada, you know that . . ."

And suddenly, Mrs. Twist stopped talking, too. She pushed her glasses up and looked closely at her young daughter's face. And at that moment, her heart also turned to goo. Ada was trying her best to tell her something. And she didn't understand what.

Mrs. Twist sighed and knelt next to Ada. She looked at her daughter and smiled kindly. She took a deep breath and let it out slowly.

"Start at the start," she said gently.

And that's what Ada did. She told her mom about the birds and the tree and how Uncle Ned flew into the—

Mrs. Twist jumped to her feet.

"What?!" she said. "Ned Revere is flying around town in helium pants? This is an emergency!"

"I know," said Ada. "But it's okay."

"What do you mean?" asked Mrs. Twist. "How is it okay?"

Ada smiled. "Because I know what to do."

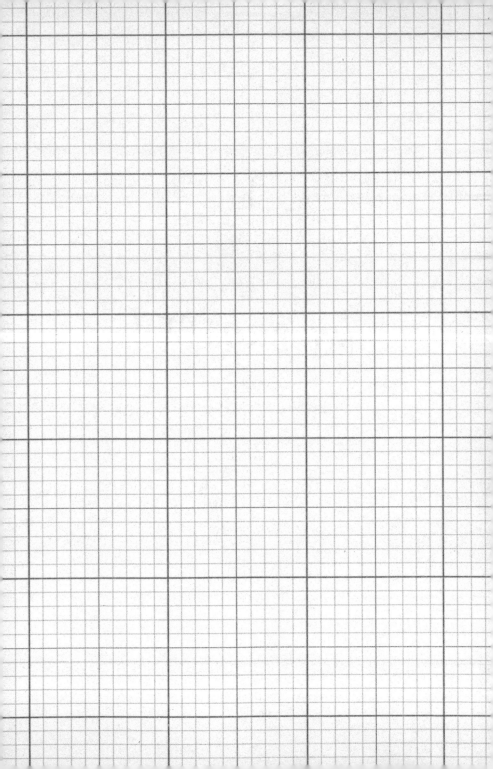

I

MY BROTHER

CHAPTER 13

Just then, Ada's brother, Arthur, came in. He pointed at the racquet.

"Is that my rac—" he started, but then interrupted himself. "Mom! There's a guy with balloon pants flying around town! I think he's in trouble!"

"We know," said Mrs. Twist.

Arthur looked at his mom. He looked at Ada. He looked at his tennis racquet, which was his most prized possession in the world.

He looked at Ada again.

"How can I help?" he asked.

CHAPTER 14

They sped back to the factory. The bus screeched to a stop and Uncle Fred pulled the lever to open the door.

"Good luck, Ada!" he said.

They hopped off the bus.

"He's still up there!" said Arthur, pointing to Uncle Ned.

The crowd was even larger now. The monkeys were racing up and down the fire ladder and an ostrich was pecking at the fire hose.

"We're back!" announced Ada.

"Helloooooo-oooooo-oooooo!" yelled Uncle Ned.

"Let's get to work," said Ada.

Arthur opened the bag of tennis balls.

Ada took out a ball and grabbed the racquet.

"What's the plan?" asked Iggy.

"I'm going to hit balls to Uncle Ned, and when he catches them, their mass will be added to his mass, and gravity will pull him toward Earth, and then the . . ." said Ada.

Iggy looked confused.

Ada started to get overwhelmed. She needed to explain, but she didn't have time to draw a picture to show the plan.

Rosie looked at Ada and smiled.

"I get it!" she said. "Uncle Ned is like a boat floating on a sea of air. You're going to weigh him down with tennis balls until his 'boat' sinks and Beau can grab him!"

"You'll overcome
the buoyancy force!"
said Iggy. "See? I got it!"

Ada beamed. Now, all she
had to do was make the plan
work!

"Put the tennis balls in your
helmet, Uncle Ned!" she yelled.

"Okay!" he yelled back. "But can
you hurry? There are two mean-looking birds on
the wall up here!"

"What do they look like?" said Ada.

"They are black and purple and have a V in

their tails," said Uncle Ned. "They are swooping at me like crazy!"

"Do they have orange beaks?" asked Ada.

"No!" yelled Uncle Ned. "They have beady eyes and a bad attitude!"

Ada thought for a moment and yelled back.

"Do you have any dragonflies in your pocket?" she asked.

"No!" cried Uncle Ned.

"Then don't worry about it," said Ada. "Those are Purple Martins, and they eat flying insects like dragonflies. They won't bother you."

"Phew-ewwww-ewwww!" replied Uncle Ned, swirling around again and again.

Ada grabbed a tennis ball and took aim.

"I need to hit it at this angle," she said, pointing up to Uncle Ned.

"That's about a hundred degrees," said Iggy. "I used an angle like that in my cheese-cracker arch the other day. It was delicious!"

THE PURPLE MARTIN
FROM *THE NERD BIRD*
GUIDE TO BIRDS FOR NERDS

By Mr. Otto Bonn

The Purple Martin

Family: Hirundinidae
Genus and Species: *Progne subis*

Swallows are slim, graceful birds that swoop and dive through the air to catch flying insects. They have pointed wings, tiny feet, and short bills which open very wide to capture insects in flight.

The Purple Martin is the largest swallow in North America. Males are purple-black on top and underneath. They are the only swallows with black bellies. The females are light in color, including their bellies and chin. Purple Martin tail feathers are shaped like the letter V.

The Purple Martin migrates each winter to South America, then returns to North America to nest in the spring. They nest in semi-open country near water, towns, and farms. In the west, they can be found in saguaro desert and mountain forests.

Purple Martins like to nest in communities. They often nest in multi-room bird houses put up by people. However, Purple Martin populations are dropping. Possibly because of a lack of nesting sites, and competition with starlings.

"Here goes," said Ada.

She swung the racquet.

THWACK!

The bright green ball flew off the racquet and right at Iggy's head. It grazed his hair. It bounced off the wall and knocked the sketching pencil out of Barb Ross's hand.

"Hey!" said Iggy. "Aim for Uncle Ned!"

"I did!" said Ada.

She tried again.

THWONK!

The ball hit the fire ladder next to a monkey. The monkey screeched at Ada, grabbed the tennis ball, and ran off.

"Sorry!" she said.

THWOOP!

THWOOP!

Ada hit ball after ball and they went everywhere EXCEPT where they were supposed to go.

Ada frowned. She was frustrated. Why didn't this work? Ada studied her notebook.

"Why isn't it working?" she asked. "I know how high to hit the ball and how hard."

"Knowing what to do isn't the same as being able to do it," said her mom.

Ada's mother was right. Ada knew all about the forces and angles, but she didn't know how to hit the balls to make it happen. There was only one person she knew who could do that. She handed the racquet to her brother.

"Can you do it?" she asked.

Arthur smiled.

"Did world-famous tennis champion Arthur Ashe wear wristbands?" he asked.

Ada knew the answer to that. Her brother had five posters of his favorite tennis player on his walls. Arthur Ashe wore wristbands in each one.

WHAT IS AN EDDY?

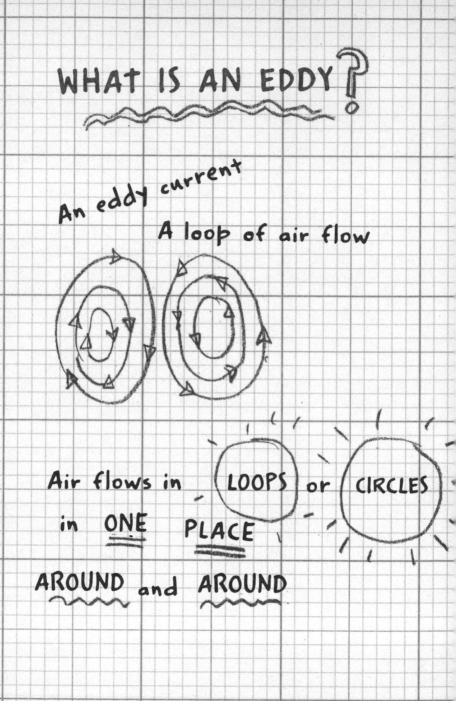

An eddy current

A loop of air flow

Air flows in LOOPS or CIRCLES

in ONE PLACE

AROUND and AROUND

CHAPTER 15

The dark clouds were looming closer and Ada could see the far-off trees swaying in the wind. A storm was coming.

Soon, that wind would reach the factory, and when it did, everything would change. The eddy that now trapped Uncle Ned would collapse and he would be set loose from its grasp. Then, who knows where he might fly?

"Hurry, Arthur!" said Ada. "We're running out of time."

Arthur grabbed a tennis ball.

THWACK!

The ball lobbed into the air and soared gently over Uncle Ned and right past him. It dropped to the ground with a gentle thud.

"Too hard," Arthur said and adjusted his grip. He tried again.

THWACK!

This time, the ball arced high into the air. Uncle Ned reached out and grabbed it! The crowd cheered. Uncle Ned took off his helmet and put the tennis ball inside.

"Keep going!" said Ada.

THWACK! THWACK! THWACK!

Arthur hit ball after ball into the air. One after another, they flew close enough for Uncle Ned to catch and put in his helmet. As Ada had hoped, Uncle Ned dropped a tiny bit lower in the air. The plan was working. The crowd went wild!

"Yay!" they cheered. "Arthur! Arthur!"

Like his favorite tennis player on Centre Court at Wimbledon, Arthur Twist took a deep breath and focused.

THWACK! THWACK! THWACK!

Arthur hit the tennis balls perfectly. Uncle Ned missed a ball, but he caught the next two. As he added each ball to the helmet, he dropped a little lower. He hovered a few centimeters out of Beau's reach. Beau stretched as far as his long arms could go.

"I can almost reach you!" yelled Beau. "Hurry, Arthur! The storm clouds are coming!"

Indeed, the dark clouds moved closer and closer still.

THWACK!

"One more!" yelled Ada.

THWACK!

With perfect precision, Arthur lobbed a ball high into the air. The ball soared up . . . up . . . up . . . and into Uncle Ned's outstretched hand.

Uncle Ned grabbed it. He plopped it onto the pile of tennis balls in the helmet.

Uncle Ned dipped toward the ladder as Beau reached and reached and reached—

HOT

HOT

HOT

HOT

HOT

HOT

↑
Heat rises up

UP
↑↑↑

Hot
asphalt

?

Hot ground

I ♥ CATS

CHAPTER 16

Just then, a large dragonfly zipped past Uncle Ned's head.

One Purple Martin spied the dragonfly and zoomed after it.

Swoosh!

The bird swooped past Uncle Ned's right ear.

Swoosh!

The other Purple Martin zoomed past Uncle Ned's left ear. They fluttered and tumbled through the air like acrobats. Just as Beau's fingertips touched the tip of Uncle Ned's shoe, the dragonfly landed on Uncle Ned's nose.

"HELP!" cried Uncle Ned, dropping the helmet and slapping at his face.

The helmet crashed to the ground. The green balls hit the steamy-hot asphalt and bounced in every direction.

Boing! Boing! Boing!

The lemurs, monkeys, and ostrich chased the balls right into the crowd. People shrieked and eeeeked! It was chaos!

Ada, Iggy, and Rosie watched in horror as Uncle Ned popped higher into the air out of Beau's reach.

"Heeeeeeeelp!" he yelled. "Do something!"

The tennis balls bounced like gas molecules spreading out in every direction! Just like the molecules that spread out from Arthur's hot, stinky shoe.

Ada remembered her experiment and what

she had learned. The hot shoe was stinkier than the cold one. At least, the stink of it had reached Ada faster than the stink of the cold shoe. That meant that the hot air molecules spread faster than the cold air molecules.

Ada quickly flipped open her notes. There it was! The answer to the problem!

Ada looked at the hot, black asphalt down below Uncle Ned. The surface sizzled and heated the air above it, which rose in gentle waves. Stinky, nose-burning, asphalt-reeking waves. And that is when Ada Marie Twist knew exactly what to do.

There was no time to lose!

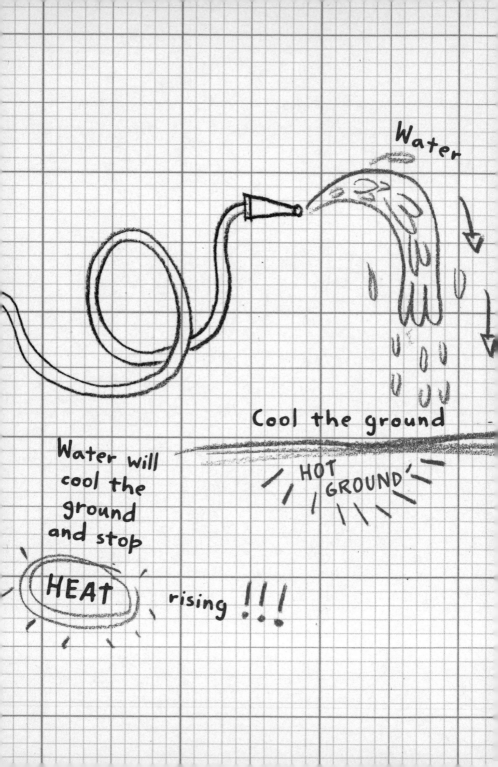

CHAPTER 17

Quick!" shouted Ada. "Grab the hose!"

Ada and Iggy ran to the fire hose, which was laying on the hot pavement next to the truck.

"No!" said Rosie. "Remember what will happen? You'll knock Uncle Ned out of the eddy and he'll fly off into that wind!"

"No, he won't," said Ada. "Trust me!"

She grabbed the end of the fire hose.

Iggy grabbed the hose behind her.

Rosie looked doubtful but jumped in line behind Iggy.

"Hit it, Bee!" yelled Ada.

Bee flipped the switch on the pumper truck and a heavy spray of water burst out of the hose. It was more powerful than Ada had imagined. The three friends struggled to control the hose, but they held tight.

"Get ready, Beau!" Ada yelled, and she pointed the hose at the asphalt just below Uncle Ned.

The water splashed over the hot surface, and instantly Uncle Ned plunged downward. It wasn't much, but it was just enough! Beau reached out and grabbed him by the foot!

Bee flipped off the water and the hose flopped to the ground. Uncle Fred scrambled up the ladder and grabbed the rope dangling from Uncle Ned's waist.

"We got him!" yelled Uncle Fred.

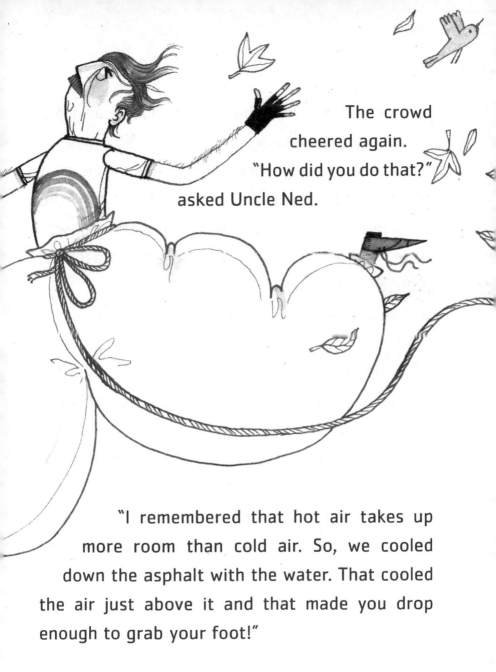

The crowd cheered again.
"How did you do that?" asked Uncle Ned.

"I remembered that hot air takes up more room than cold air. So, we cooled down the asphalt with the water. That cooled the air just above it and that made you drop enough to grab your foot!"

"Well done!" said Uncle Ned. "Now can I get out of these pants?"

But there was no time. Just then, a strong gust of wind blasted into the courtyard and blew the dust and leaves up and away. The whirlwind was gone. A heavy raindrop splattered the asphalt. Then another. And another.

Raindrops began to fall faster and faster and the crowd scattered. Uncle Fred tied Uncle Ned's rope to the bumper of the Zoo Bus and rounded up the zoo animals. The Questioneers and Ada's mom and brother hopped onto the bus.

In a few moments, Uncle Fred stopped at the Twist house on Milk Lane.

"Thank you for rescuing me!" said Uncle Ned. "If it weren't for you, I'd be eaten by birds and halfway to Timbuktu by now!"

"You're welcome!" said Ada as she waved goodbye to Uncle Ned, Uncle Fred, Iggy, and Rosie.

Uncle Fred honked and headed down the street with Uncle Ned floating above the Zoo Bus.

Arthur ran up the steps to the front porch of the Twist house. Ada and Mrs. Twist followed him as thunder rumbled in the distance.

"Thanks for letting me use your racquet," said Ada. "You could be a tennis champion someday. Like Arthur Ashe."

"Maybe," said Arthur. "But you should stick with science."

Arthur opened the front door and stepped into the house. He paused and smiled at Ada.

"Actually," he said. "Let me know if you want to play tennis sometime. You weren't that bad. But you have to use your own racquet. And stay out of my stuff!"

Arthur tried to look mad, but it didn't work. Ada grinned at her brother as he shut the door, leaving Ada and her mom alone on the porch.

Just then, the sky opened up and rain poured buckets onto the roof of the porch and splashed into puddles in the yard. The smell of the rain hit Ada's nose and she closed her eyes for a moment and breathed it in. It was not the kind of smell that curled her toes. It was a warm and cozy smell that mixed with her mom's perfume and was one of the best things in the world.

Ada and her mom sat and watched the rain plop and splop and splash on the grass. Her mother put her arm around Ada and gave her a hug.

"Ada," she said. "I'm sorry I didn't listen to you when you tried to tell me about Uncle Ned. I just didn't get it."

Ada smiled at her mom.

"I know," said Ada.

"You know I'm very proud of you," said Mrs. Twist. "And I—"

"I know," said Ada.

"How do you know what I'm going to tell you?" asked Mrs. Twist.

"Because you already did," said Ada.

THINGS MOM TELLS ME

1. The bathroom is not a science lab.

2. The pantry is not an ant farm.

3. Don't put my toothbrush in the earthworm box.

4. Don't take Arthur's things.

5. I LOVE YOU.

Ada smiled. "See," she said. "I always write down the important things so I'll remember. But I have a question."

"Just one?" asked Mrs. Twist.

"Well . . ." said Ada. "Do big raindrops taste different than little ones?" she asked. "And, why is rain gray in the air but clear on my hand? Why do earthworms crawl on the sidewalk in the rain? What if . . ."

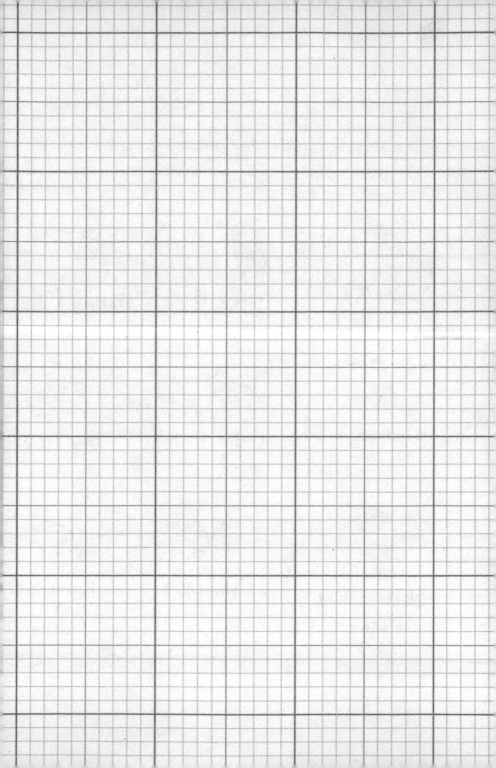

Bird count

Magpie X 6

Crow x 13

Starling X 3

Woodpecker X 1

Purple finch X 5

Blue jay X 17

Black-capped
chickadee
X 3

Wren X 3

Pigeon X 17

CITIZEN SCIENCE!

When Ada Twist performed her stink experiment, she tried to gather as much information as she could. Gathering data is how scientists test their hypotheses and learn more about the subjects they study. Sometimes, scientists need help gathering data. That's when they call on citizen scientists!

Citizen scientists are people like you who help in scientific research. Citizen scientists gather data about animals, climate, aging, botany, and many other topics.

The Great Backyard Bird Count is one example of citizen science at work. Each February, more than one hundred thousand people of all ages from around the world join in! They count and identify the birds near them and share the data they collect.

The Great Backyard Bird Count gives scientists a snapshot of the world's bird populations. Scientists use the data to learn more about weather and climate change, bird diseases, and migration.

You can learn how to join in at GBBC .birdcount.org.

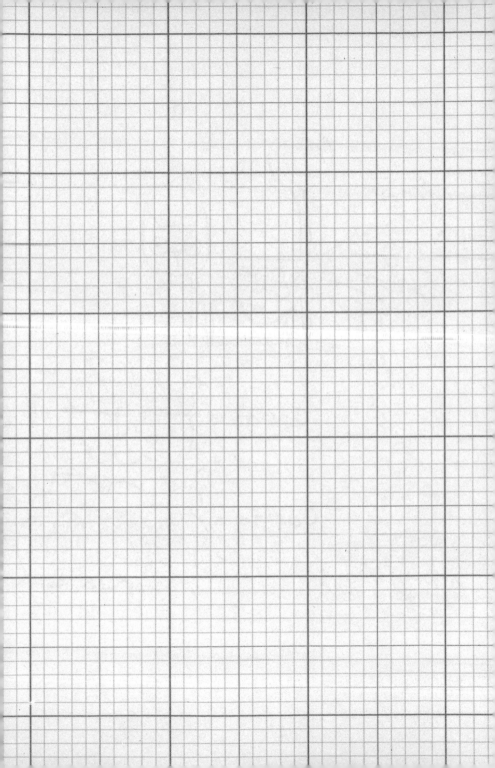

ODE TO A GAS!

What is a gas?
It's mostly just space
with a few molecules bouncing all over the place.
They bounce faster and farther when the
    temperature's hot.
They slow and condense when the temperature
    is not.
Compared to a solid, there's nothing much to it,
so most of the time, you can see right through it.

Some gases fill caverns deep underground.
Some gases fill the sky.
Some gases fill your tummy and no matter how
    you try
they sneak out and make a sound.
It's embarrassing—but alas!—
it's part of being human. And in the end,
this too shall pass.

THAT'S FOR THE BIRDS!

Ada Twist loves science. She loves studying nature. Because of that, she spends a lot of time observing animals. Especially birds!

There are many reasons to study birds:

- Birds have played a role in art and mythology, music, and culture since ancient times.
- Studying birds helps us understand the planet and nature. For instance, studying finches in the Galapagos Islands shaped Charles Darwin's understanding of natural selection in evolution.
- Birds are a food source wherever there are people. There are about twenty-three billion chickens on the planet!
- Birds live almost everywhere on Earth and they travel almost everywhere

on Earth. The Arctic Tern (*Sterna paradisaea*) migrates each year from the Arctic to Antarctica and back again! That is a lot of flying.

- There are about 10,000 species of birds on our planet. More than 1,400 of them are threatened with extinction. Understanding birds can help us know how to help them.

- Forty percent of bird species have populations that are declining!

- Birds pollinate plants and distribute seeds. They help maintain variety in plant species, which also fosters variety in animal species. This variety is called biodiversity. Bird populations mirror the health of other animal and plant populations. Studying birds helps us understand the health of our planet!

- Bird populations respond to environmental changes. Both good changes and bad ones.

- Populations decline because of lack of food, destruction of nesting grounds, and pollution. Changes in climate can also affect where and when birds migrate. Birds might migrate early because of warmer temperatures, but the seeds or insects they need for food might not be available at the earlier time. Birds could starve in this case.
- A drop in bird populations often reflects a drop in insect, mammal, reptile, and other animal populations.
- We require biodiversity to have good sources of food and quality air and water. Without these things, humans cannot survive on Earth!

THINK ABOUT THIS . . .

Unless you grow it yourself, everything you eat comes from somewhere else. That might be a place close by, or it might be from the other side of our planet. Even snack foods might have ingredients from many places. In either case, product ingredients and their transportation and packaging have a big impact on the environment and animals, including birds.

One ingredient that is commonly used in packaged foods is palm oil. Palm oil trees are found in North and South America, Asia, and Africa. They are grown on plantations. Some plantations use good, sustainable growing methods. However, an enormous amount of native rainforest is burned to make room for palm oil plantations.

This is very bad for our planet, because the rainforest is home to almost half of the Earth's species of animals and plants. Rainforest destruction ruins habitats for birds and other animals like orangutans that are threatened by extinction.

The trees of the world's rainforests take carbon dioxide out of the air and add oxygen to the atmosphere. When the trees are destroyed, the carbon dioxide stays in the atmosphere. Even worse, when the trees are burned, they release an enormous amount of carbon dioxide. This carbon dioxide traps heat in the atmosphere and warms the planet.

This warming of our planet is causing climate changes that are shrinking glaciers and changing weather patterns, which makes for stronger storms and higher ocean levels. Rising ocean levels and warming temperatures are a threat to millions of people's homes and food sources.

What can you do about it?

Read the labels of food and other products including shampoo and cleaners to see if they contain palm oil.

Do some research to see if the product makers use sustainable sources for palm oil. Hint: A librarian is a great person to help you! Share what you learn with your friends and family. Learn about some groups who are working to stop destruction of the rainforest.

What actions can you take and what changes on your part can make a positive difference?

ACKNOWLEDGMENTS

From the moment an idea pops into our heads until a reader opens a book on a cozy couch somewhere, so many people add their talents and energy to make these books the best they can be.

We want to say thanks to all the librarians, educators, and parents who share our stories with the kids in their lives. Thanks to the independent booksellers who bring our books into your beautiful shops and share your enthusiasm and love for reading with everyone who comes through your door. Thanks to all the people who sell, market, distribute, and publicize the books and everyone involved in the design, production, business, and legal parts of the process.

There are indeed many, many people who show their love for these books through their hard work. Thank you, Abrams Family!

A special thanks to Erica Finkel, Andrew Smith, Chad W. Beckerman, Courtney Code, Jody Mosley, Amy Vreeland, Erin Vandeveer, Hana Anouk Nakamura, Hallie Patterson, Liz Fithian, Melanie Chang, Trish McNamara O'Neill, Jenny Choy, Elisa Gonzalez, Mary Wowk, Wendy Cellabos and Michael Jacobs.

Thank you, Rebecca Sherman and everyone at Writers House. Thank you, Christine Isteed and Artist Partners Ltd.

Thanks to Christopher Williams, Michael Uram, Katie Uram, and Andrew Uram. Thank you also to Jason Wells, Nicole Russo, and Tamar Brazis. And thank you, forever, to Susan Van Metre without whom none of this would have ever happened.

Andrea loves cheese.

David loves hats and cats (and cakes).

$$\frac{AB}{DR} + A = RRRR$$

ABOUT THE AUTHOR

ANDREA BEATY is the bestselling author of the Questioneers series, as well as the novels *Dorko the Magnificent*, *Secrets of the Cicada Summer*, and *Attack of the Fluffy Bunnies*. She has a degree in biology and computer science and spent many years in the computer industry. She now writes children's books in her home outside Chicago.

ABOUT THE ILLUSTRATOR

DAVID ROBERTS has illustrated many books, including the Questioneers series, *The Cook and the King*, and *Happy Birthday, Madame Chapeau*. He lives in London, where, when not drawing, he likes to make hats.

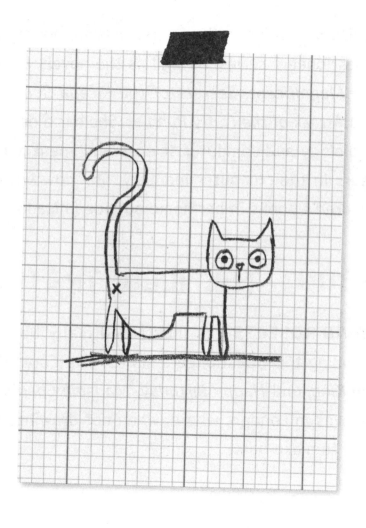

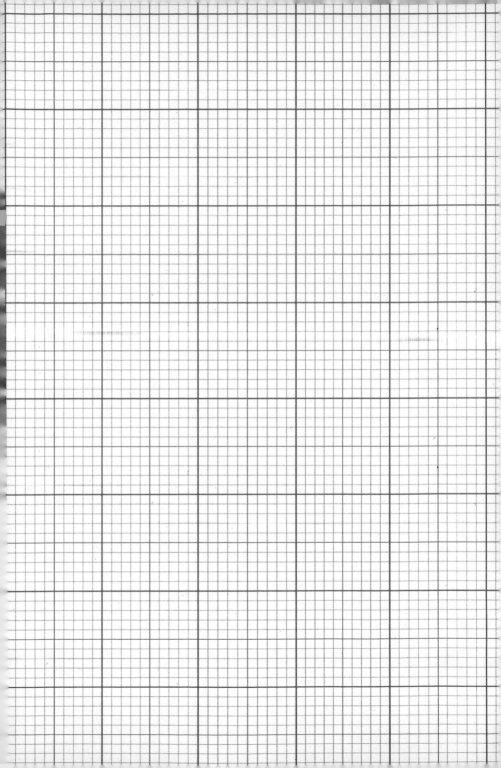

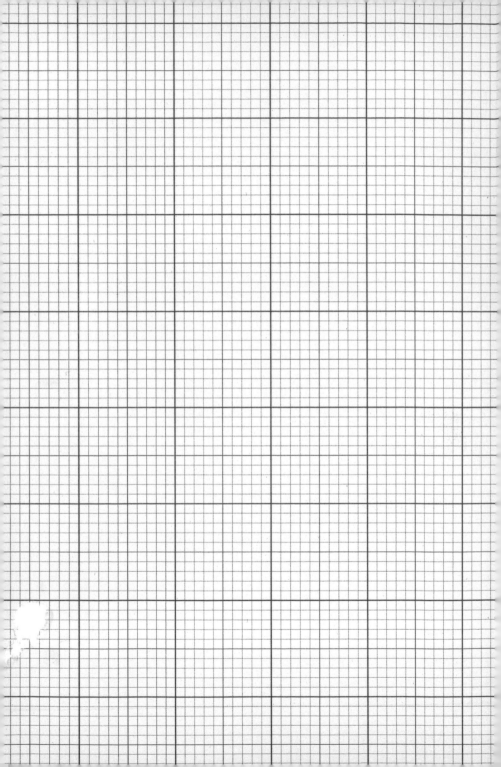